AF594833

BIOMIMICRY

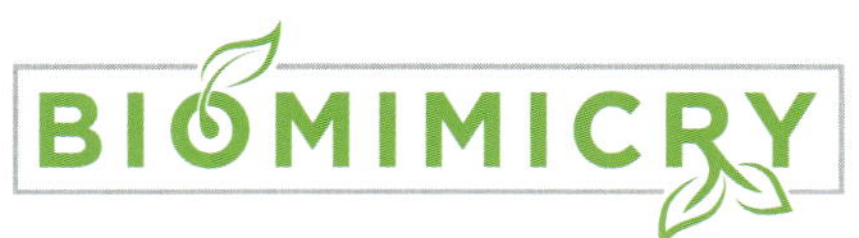

# AWESOME INNOVATIONS INSPIRED BY SHARKS

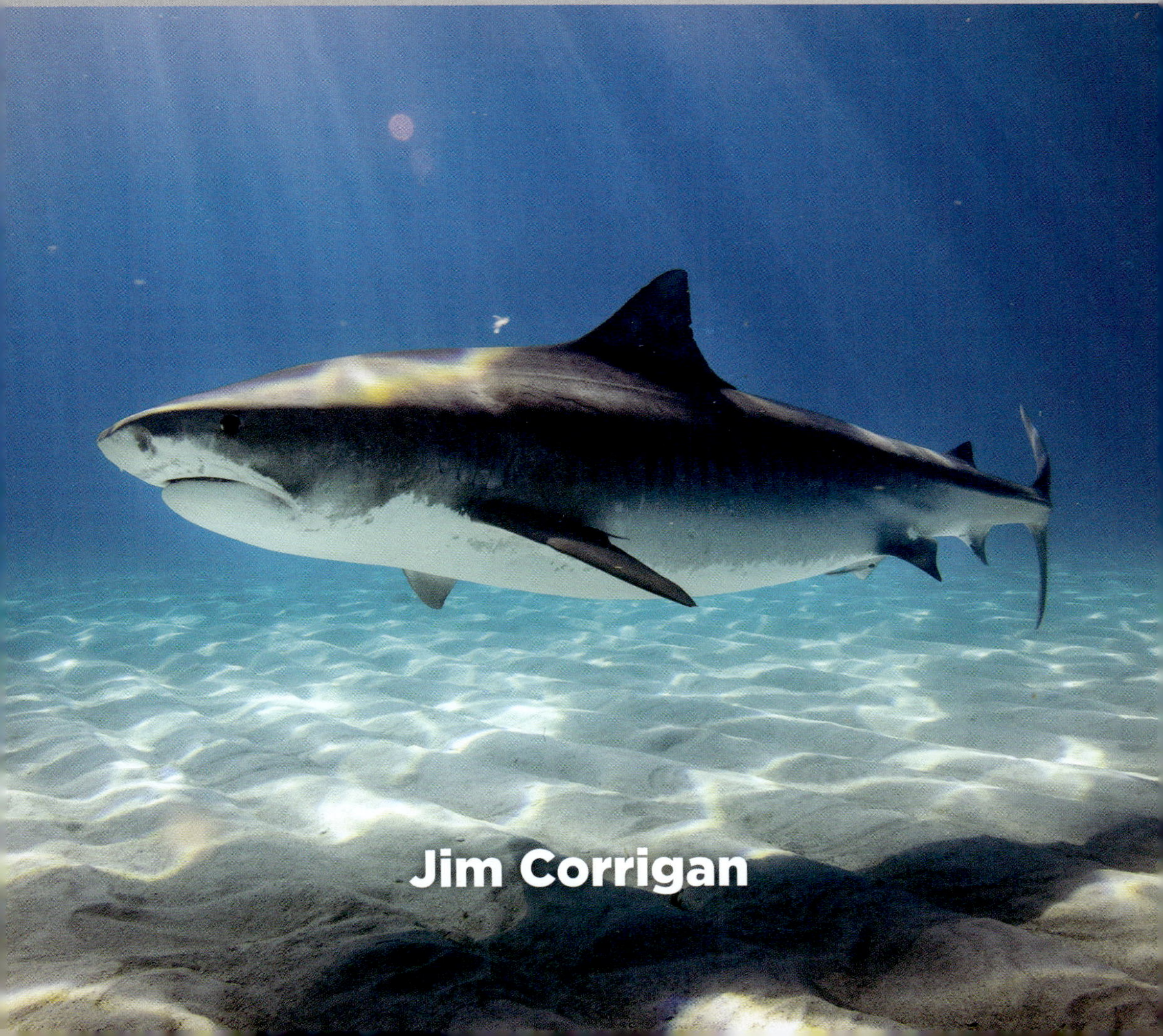

Jim Corrigan

PUBLISHERS

mitchelllane.com

2001 SW 31st Avenue
Hallandale, FL 33009

First Edition, 2021.
Author: Jim Corrigan
Designer: Ed Morgan
Editor: Sharon F. Doorasamy

Series: Biomimicry
Title: Awesome Innovations Inspired by Sharks / by Jim Corrigan

Hallandale, FL : Mitchell Lane Publishers, [2021]

Library bound ISBN: 978-1-68020-609-8
eBook ISBN: 978-1-68020-610-4

PHOTO CREDITS: cover: Gerald Schömbs on Unsplash, pp. 4-5 Gerald Schömbs on Unsplash, p. 5 Gregory S. Paulson Cultura/Newscom, p. 6 Robert A. Martin/MCT/Newscom, p. 9 Jakob Owens on Unsplash, pp. 10-11 VICTOR HABBICK VISIONS/SCIENCE PHOTO LIBRARY/Newscom, p. 12 Clint Patterson on Unsplash, p. 15 WILL BURGESS/REUTERS/ Newscom, pp. 16-17 rejohnson71 CC BY-SA 2.0 pp. 18-19 Chevrolet press photo scan, p. 21 U.S. Navy, p. 23 Danita Delimont Photography/Newscom, p. 25 Alamy

# Contents

# Skin Deep

**If you were to pet a shark,** it would feel rough. Sharks have skin like sandpaper. In the year 2000, a professor named Anthony Brennan delved deep into shark skin.

Brennan was working on a project for the U.S. Navy. The Navy needed a better way to keep algae from growing on its ships. Brennan believed shark skin might hold the answer.

Denticles make some sharks swim faster and easier than other fish.

Most fish have scales, but sharks are covered in tiny points called **denticles**. Under a microscope, denticles look like jagged teeth. Brennan suspected that denticles keep sharks free of algae and barnacles. Whales, which have smooth skin, end up with many tiny hitchhikers.

He asked a fisherman to catch a shark and make a mold of its skin, then let it go. Brennan used the mold to make fake shark skin. His lab tests showed algae could not stick to the denticles.

## chapter one

A new barnacle-killing coating is being applied to a ship in Charleston, South Carolina.

Most ship companies use harmful chemicals to prevent algae. Brennan's discovery proved there is another way. When someone finds a better way to do something, it's called **innovation**. Innovators like Anthony Brennan change the world with advances in science and technology.

## Safe Surfaces

Today, Brennan is chairman of Sharklet Technologies. The company makes a peel-and-stick film to stop germs. Germy surfaces can include food trays, checkout counters, and airport kiosks. The protective film, which copies shark skin, makes it harder for germs to stick.

When innovators borrow ideas from nature, it's called **biomimicry**. (*Bio* means "life" and *mimic* means "to copy.")

Hospitals do their best to fight germs, but it's an uphill battle. Injury opens the door to infection. Invisible bacteria lurk near wounded skin, trying to get inside the body. Every year in U.S. hospitals alone, 1.7 million patients pick up an infection.

Sharklet film helps slow the spread of bacteria in hospitals. The company also makes bandages and other medical supplies. More shark-inspired health care products are on the way.

"Nature provides so many amazing designs for us to build off of as humans," said Brennan. "I figure, Mother Nature has figured things out, so I'm going to learn as much as I can from her."

# Perfect Predator

**Sharks may be scary,** but other creatures are far more deadly. Each year, more than 100,000 people die from venomous snake bites. The pesky mosquito spreads deadly diseases. Mosquito bites result in 750,000 deaths per year. How many people do sharks kill each year? About six.

Still, the thought of a shark attack terrifies us. Humans are slow and helpless in the ocean. We cannot see through the murk. Sharks, on the other hand, glide with grace and speed. They can sense prey from far away. They are the perfect predator.

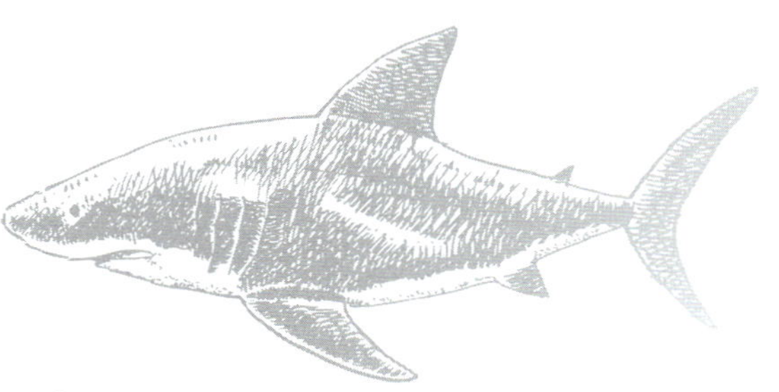

## chapter two

### Ancient Hunters

Primitive sharks appeared long before dinosaurs. Modern sharks evolved about 100 million years ago. The extinct species C. megalodon was the largest fish that ever lived. Megalodon was roughly the size of an 18-wheel truck. Each tooth was larger than a cell phone. Megalodon ate whales, dolphins, and anything else it wanted.

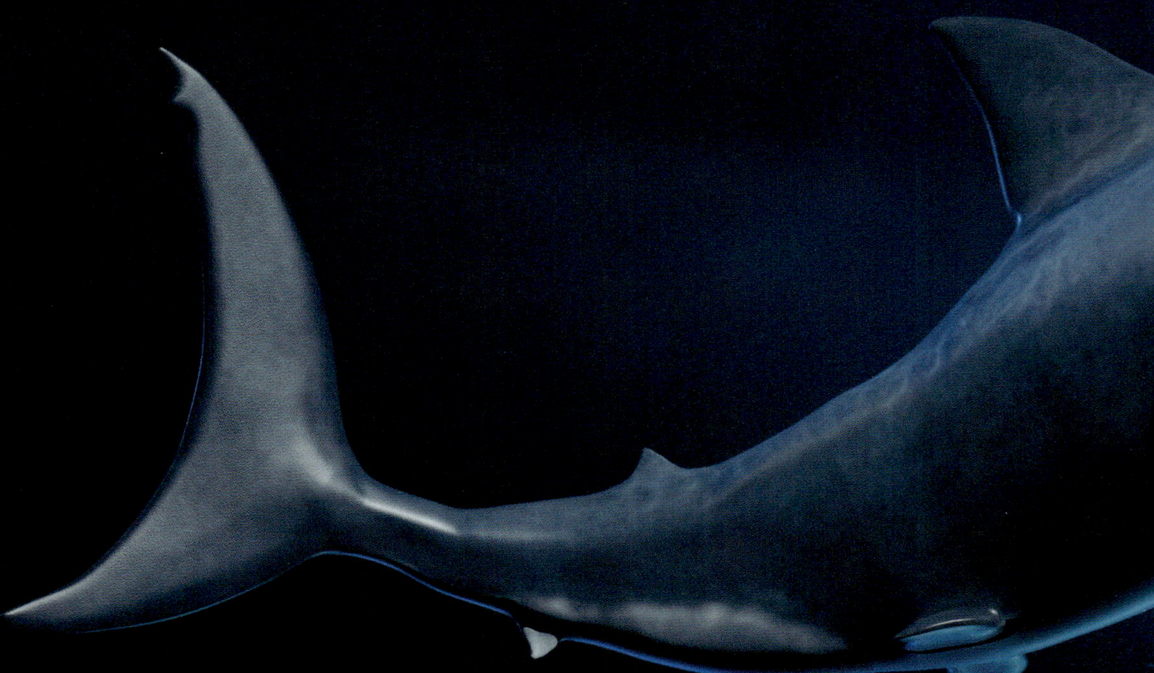

# Perfect Predator

Scientists estimate that megalodon's size falls into the 60-70 foot range, while the largest living shark, the great white, maxes out at about 21 feet. Above, an artist's illustration compares the two.

# chapter two

A shark may grow more than 20,000 teeth in its lifetime!

Sharks lose their teeth on a regular basis. New rows of sharp teeth grow along their jaws, ready to take over. Sharks find their prey by smell, sound, sight, and vibration.

They also have a sense called **electro-reception**. All animals create a small electric field when they move their muscles. Sharks can sense these signals. When a fish flexes its muscles to swim, sharks can feel it. An injured, flopping fish will send out large signals. Sharks come looking for the easy meal.

Alexis Abramson is an engineering professor at Case Western Reserve University. She studies the special gel that enables sharks to sense electricity. Abramson believes that mimicking the gel could spur many new innovations. For example, someday we might be able to turn the waste heat from a car engine into usable electricity.

Biomimicry is not a new concept. Since 1997, a science writer named Janine Benyus has been urging innovators to look to nature for great ideas. Benyus wrote a book titled *Biomimicry: Innovation Inspired by Nature*. She noted that many plants and animals have already solved the problems we find so vexing. Plus, natural solutions do not harm the environment.

Sharks, with their special abilities and senses, offer many exciting chances for biomimicry.

**Shark attacks always make big news, but they are very rare. In the United States, the odds of being killed by a shark are 3,748,067 to 1.**

# Clever Copies

**In the Olympics,** swim races come down to just fractions of a second. A slight edge can separate victory from defeat. In 2000, the swimsuit company Speedo mimicked shark skin. Its Fastskin suit stirred a controversy.

The 2000 Summer Olympics took place in Sydney, Australia. Some swimmers showed up wearing Fastskin suits, which covered them from wrist to ankle. The suit's fabric had tiny, V-shaped ridges, much like shark denticles. Speedo said it was more efficient in water than bare skin.

The suits made a huge difference. More than 80 percent of the medal winners wore a Fastskin. They broke 13 records. Swimsuit companies raced to make even faster full-body suits. More records soon fell.

Australian swimmer Susie O'Neill models the Speedo Fastskin.

Racing officials finally banned high-tech swimsuits in 2009. They said the suits gave swimmers an unfair advantage, like wearing flippers. But the story didn't end there.

In 2012, a Harvard professor named George Lauder tested the Fastskin fabric. He found that the suit's success did not come from mimicking shark skin. Denticles do help agile sharks swim faster, Lauder said. But they do nothing for clunky humans.

Full-body suits helped only because they were so tight. They squeezed the human body into a more **streamlined** shape. Today, rules limit how far a suit may cover a swimmer's body.

## Shark Art

Sharks capture our imagination. We fear them but also admire their strength and grace. Many artists have celebrated the menacing beauty of sharks.

A Texas-based artist named Robbie Barber bought used golf bags at flea markets and thrift stores. Barber turned each bag into a shark. His golf-bag creations included great whites, hammerheads, and blue sharks. He placed them together in a display called *The Reef*.

Artist Kitty Wales decided to go see sharks for herself. She went diving in the Bahamas, sketching on a plastic slate as curious sharks swam by.

Once home in Massachusetts, Wales sculpted three sharks using old household appliances. She made one shark from an oil burner. Another came from refrigerator parts. Wales crafted the third shark out of scraps from a kitchen stove.

Both artists used junk for a reason. They were pointing out our harmful impact on nature. Every year, more than 8 million tons of plastic and other trash end up in the ocean.

Kitty Wales named her outdoor installation at DeCordova Sculpture Park in Massachusetts "Pine Sharks."

In 1961, General Motors unveiled the XP-755 Mako Shark. The concept car had a sleek nose with side vents that looked like gills. A blue-gray paint job faded to white on the sides, mimicking a real mako shark. Many of the XP-755's stylish features would be used in the Chevrolet Corvette.

# Robot Sharks

**Few predators** are as stealthy as a shark. In 2019, a Chinese company made Robo-Shark. The company, Boya Gongdao, built the sea drone for China's navy.

Robo-Shark looks like a plump, little shark. Its tail is more efficient than a propeller. Plus, it is much quieter. The drone can sneak into heavily guarded waters on spy missions. Robo-Shark also has sonar for tracking enemy drones and divers.

Many nations are experimenting with shark-inspired robots. The U.S. Navy's GhostSwimmer drone has been on the prowl since 2014. The European Defence Agency is building an entire team of sea drones. They would work together during spy missions.

GhostSwimmer is designed to look and swim like a real fish.

## Energy Inventions

Some companies mimic sharks to make electricity. BioPower Systems of Sydney, Australia, makes an energy-producing shark tail.

The fake tail is anchored to the sea floor. It sways back and forth, driven by water currents. An attached generator turns that motion into electricity. Swift water currents make the shark tail sway faster, meaning more electricity.

Meanwhile, inventor Anthony Reale took inspiration from a specific shark. The Michigan native copied the basking shark for his **water turbine**. Although big and ugly, the basking shark is harmless. This enormous **filter feeder** swims with its mouth open, scooping up plankton.

The basking shark has a highly efficient filter. As it swims, water enters its mouth and passes through special gills that nearly encircle its head. An adult can filter up to 500 tons of water per hour.

Anthony Reale's turbine mimics the basking shark's filter. It features an opening inside an opening. Water passes through both openings, creating suction. The design is 40 percent more efficient than traditional water turbines.

Some researchers study a common shark sidekick, the remora. Also known as the suckerfish, it latches onto a shark's body. The remora gets a free ride and some leftover food scraps, but it does not harm the shark.

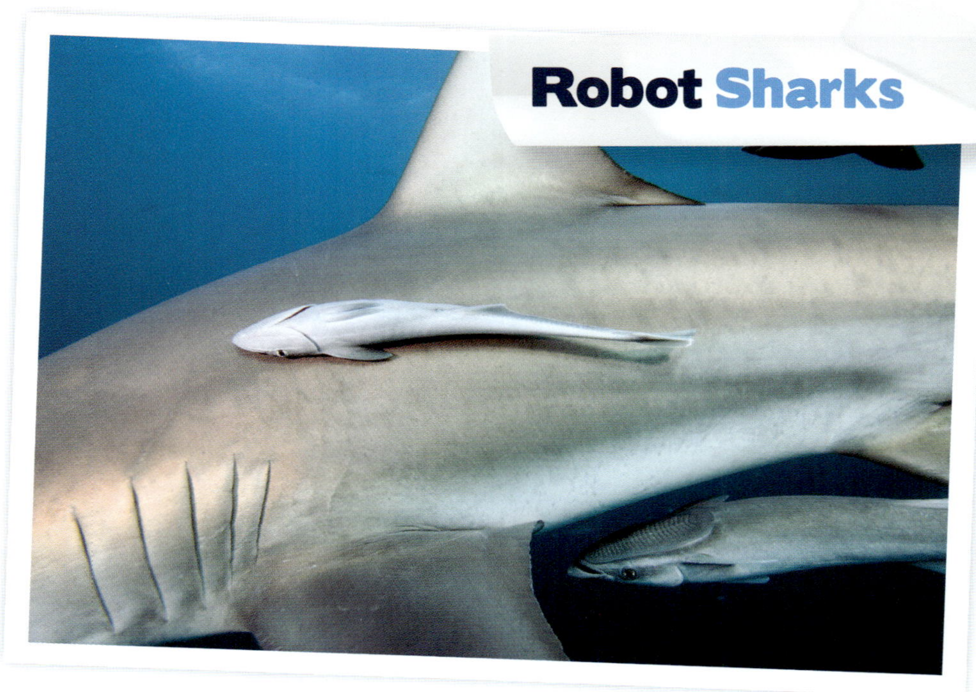


Remoras are found in tropical waters.

How do remoras cling to sandpapery shark skin? With a powerful suction disk on its belly. In 2019, researchers at the New Jersey Institute of Technology mimicked remora suction disks. They used a 3D printer to make close copies.

Their research may lead to products that stick well but let go easily. Imagine a band-aid that comes off without hurting.

**Shark livers contain an oil called squalene that is used in lipstick, lotions, and sunscreen. Millions of deep-sea sharks die each year for this reason. A company called SynShark has found a way to get squalene from tobacco plants. The technology will save sharks and help tobacco farmers as smoking declines.**

# Glowing Future

**A tiny shark** prowls the dark depths of the Gulf of Mexico. As it swims, the pocket shark emits a trail of glowing fluid. Little fish are drawn to the strange streak of light. In an instant, they become the pocket shark's dinner.

Scientists discovered the American pocket shark in 2013. It is one of the rarest animals in the world. Biologists know of just one other pocket shark. It was found off the coast of Chile in 1979.

Many other deep-sea fish also use light. In the inky depths, glow-in-the-dark tricks can be highly effective. Creatures use light to attract prey and find a mate.

In 2019, scientists studied two types of glowing sharks: the swell shark and the chain catshark. Both give off a bright green hue. The study revealed a special **molecule** in their skin. Mimicking this molecule could help doctors find cancer cells in the human body.

The study did not end there. Further analysis showed that the molecule does more than just glow. It also appears to protect sharks from disease. Exactly how this molecule works is still a mystery. It offers tremendous hope for biomimicry.

Chain catsharks, like the one pictured here, are among at least 200 marine species known to light up the oceanic world.

## Super Sniffers

Many predators have a good sense of smell, but sharks are super sniffers. They can detect the faintest scent from great distances.

Not only that, a shark can tell which of its two nostrils picked up the scent first. This clue tells it whether to turn left or right. A shark's ability to "smell in stereo" leads it directly to the odor's source. Hammerheads, with their distant nostrils, excel at this task.

Sharks smell through a pair of nostril-like holes called nares. Smell is so vital to a shark that two-thirds of its brain is devoted to it.

Boston University researchers say we might be able to give the same skill to robots. It would be especially useful for oil-hunting sea drones.

Oil pipelines run along the seabed for hundreds of miles. When one springs a leak, it can be hard to find, even for a fleet of high-tech drones. The robots might have more success if they could sniff out oil drops the same way sharks find prey.

Each year, 1.3 million gallons (4.9 million liters) of oil are spilled in U.S. waters alone. Someday, shark-inspired drones might help lessen the damage.

Biomimicry is the act of copying nature to solve human problems. Natural solutions do not harm the environment. With biomimicry, people in science and business are finding tomorrow's ideas today.

# What You Should Know

**Shark skin has tiny, tooth-like points called denticles, which prevent algae and barnacles.** Some hospitals use a denticle-inspired film to keep germs from clinging to surfaces.

**Sharks can sense the faint electrical signals** given off by living creatures. They can also **smell an odor from far away,** then find its source by telling **which nostril picked up the scent first.**

**Many navies are experimenting with sea drones that look and swim like sharks.** They are quieter and more efficient than traditional drones.

**Some deep-sea sharks can glow in the dark.** Researchers believe glowing shark skin can help us find many innovations in science and medicine.

**The smart ideas that come from biomimicry have an extra benefit.** They are safe for the environment.

# Want to be an engineer? Architect? Inventor?

1. **Take math** and **science** classes
2. **Enroll in art** and **design** classes
3. **Attend STEM** camps and programs
4. **Visit nature preserves** and **parks** to observe nature at work
5. **Keep a journal** or a **blog** of your observations
6. **Enter science fairs** and **competitions**
7. **Check out books** on **biomimicry** from your school and public library
8. **Visit natural history museums** and **science centers**
9. **Check your community's calendar** for talks by **science** and **technology experts**
10. **Volunteer for citizen science events** like **bird counts**, **water sample collection**, and **weather reporting**

# Glossary

**biomimicry**
Borrowing ideas from nature

**denticle**
A small tooth or tooth-like object

**electro-reception**
The detection of electric fields or currents

**filter feeder**
An animal that feeds on tiny bits strained out of the water

**innovation**
To create or improve an object or method

**molecule**
The smallest unit of a substance that has all the properties of that substance

**streamlined**
Shaped to offer the least possible resistance to a current of air, water, etc.

**water turbine**
An engine that turns the flow of water into energy

# Online Resources

**Visit the Conservationist for Kids webpage**
www.dec.ny.gov/education/40248.html for more information about: Biomimicry, Green Chemistry, Green Schools, and Sustainability

**Check out the Ask Nature website**
www.asknature.org

**Listen to Janine Benyus talk about biomimicry**
www.ted.com/speakers/janine_benyus

**Learn more about citizen science projects**
www.nationalgeographic.org/idea/citizen-science-projects

**Visit the Patents and Trademarks of Biomimicry**
www.uspto.gov/kids/Biomimicry.pdf

**Dive into the shadowy world of the great white shark**
kids.nationalgeographic.com/animals/fish/great-white-shark/

# Further Reading


Becker, Helaine, and Alex Ries. *Zoobots: Wild Robots Inspired by Real Animals*. Tonawanda, NY: Kids Can Press, 2014.

Harman, Jay. *The Shark's Paintbrush: Biomimicry and How Nature Is Inspiring Innovation*. Ashland, OR: White Cloud Press, 2014.

Harvey, Derek. *Sharks and Other Deadly Ocean Creatures: Visual Encyclopedia*. New York: DK Children, 2016.

Koontz, Robin. *Nature-Inspired Contraptions*. North Mankato, MN: Rourke Educational Media, 2018.

# Index

# About the Author

**Jim Corrigan** has been writing nonfiction for more than 20 years. He holds degrees from Penn State and Johns Hopkins. Jim became a fan of biomimicry while working on a book about airplanes. He currently lives near Philadelphia.